Milo makes a new friend…

The thing followed Milo, emerging from the water like a demon rising from Beneath.

Milo's mouth dropped open as he stared at the creature. It was a *sea monster*. A sea monster that walked!

It stood a few feet taller than Milo. Its body was humanlike, but scaly and dark, and it had claw hands and dragon wings and its face was a mass of tentacles beneath two huge red eyes.

An octo-dragon, Milo thought. *Awesome.*

One of the tentacles reached out and touched Milo. He giggled.

The creature made a gurgling sound in return.

"Hi," the boy said, holding out his hand to shake. "I'm Milo."

The squid-head cocked to one side and looked at the hand. "Mrrr... oh?" it chirped.

"Close enough," Milo said. The creature apparently didn't want to shake, so he took his hand back. "What's your name?"

The beast said nothing. It looked at Milo curiously, like it was deciding how best to cook him…

What happens next???

CTHULHU 4 KIDS

BOOK I

OLD ONES AT THE BEACH

by Luke J. Morris

Illustrated by Mo Simpson

An Eyeteeth Enterprises publication

Cthulhu 4 Kids: Old Ones at the Beach

Text © 2013 by Luke J. Morris

Illustrations © 2013 by Michael O. Simpson

This is a work of fiction. Any resemblance herein to real beings living, dead, or dwelling in an extradimensional plane of existence, is purely coincidental.

Cthulhu, R'lyeh, and the Old Ones are creations of H.P. Lovecraft

For Miles,

the next monster-tamer

And for H.P. Lovecraft,

the greatest of all monster-makers

"Vacation time," Milo's Dad said. "Let's go to the beach!"

"Yay!" Milo said, clapping his hands. The beach was exciting. Its sand hid all sorts of cool treasures, and Milo loved to play in the water.

The family hopped in the car and headed out. On the way to the beach Milo and his Mom sang songs while Dad hummed along. They sang 'The Itsy-Bitsy Spider', 'A-Hunting We Will Go', and 'Down by the Bay'.

Milo also belted out his own song, 'When the Old Ones Rise':

When the Old Ones rise

(clap, clap, clap, clap)

They will change the tides

(clap, clap, clap, clap)

They will eat this world

(clap, clap, clap, clap)

Every boy and girl

(clap, clap, clap, clap)

And so on, for twelve more verses. Mom didn't know the words to that one, but she sang and clapped along as best she could.

"That's one talented boy we have there," Dad said.

"He sure is," Mom replied, smiling back at Milo.

At last they arrived at the beach. Mom and Dad pulled the blanket and towels and umbrellas out of the car. Milo got out and raced into the water, laughing and shouting the whole way.

Then he met the octopus thing.

At first he just saw its eyeballs above the water.

Those eyes stared at Milo like they wanted to devour him, which made him a little uncomfortable. He stepped back onto the sand.

The thing followed Milo, emerging from the water like a demon rising from Beneath.

Milo's mouth dropped open as he stared at the creature. It was a *sea monster*. A sea monster that walked!

It stood a few feet taller than Milo. Its body was humanlike, but scaly and dark, and it had claw hands and dragon wings and its face was a mass of tentacles beneath two huge red eyes.

An octo-dragon, Milo thought. *Awesome.*

One of the tentacles reached out and touched Milo. He giggled.

The creature made a gurgling sound in return.

"Hi," the boy said, holding out his hand to shake. "I'm Milo."

The squid-head cocked to one side and looked at the hand. "Mrrr... oh?" it chirped.

"Close enough," Milo said. The creature apparently didn't want to shake, so he took his hand back. "What's your name?"

The beast said nothing. It looked at Milo curiously, like it was deciding how best to cook him.

Milo pointed at the thing's chest. "What do I call you?"

The creature made a few clicking noises. Then it placed its claw on its chest and gurgled, "Keh...Too...Loo..."

Milo scrunched his nose. That name was too hard to pronounce. "I'll call you Kulu," he decided. "Want to play?"

Kulu looked confused for a minute. Then it shrugged and nodded.

The boy smiled. "Yay! Let's build sandcastles."

The sea monster stared at him blankly.

"It's easy!" Milo said. "Here, I'll show you."

Milo sat in the wet sand and started to build.

First he pressed sand together in a round pile. Next he flattened it out on top to form a turret. He put notches on its roof and windows in its walls.

Kulu watched Milo with interest.

After a couple minutes Milo looked up. "Aren't you

going to help?" he asked. Friends weren't much good if they wouldn't play.

He (Milo thought for sure Kulu was a 'he') looked at Milo's turret for a moment more. Then his monstrous eyes popped wide open, he raised his claw hands before him, and a massive turret exploded from the sand next to Milo's miniature one.

"Cool!" Milo said. He started building walls to connect the turrets, so Kulu did that too.

Soon they'd made a whole medieval city of sand. It had a large castle in the center, a main road between the buildings of town, an outer wall, and a moat.

The place was so big, Milo could have *lived* in it. In fact, he wanted to.

"This is great!" Milo said. "What should we call it?"

Kulu rested his tentacled head in his claws like he was thinking. "R'lyeh?" he said at last.

"Riley?" Milo shrugged. "I guess that works."

Milo got up and walked to the water. He turned around and looked at the city he and his new friend had built, and he smiled. It was a beautiful metropolis of brown buildings, formed in twisted shapes that didn't belong on Earth. Milo felt proud.

Then Kulu dove into the water and disappeared.

Milo gasped. He ran to Kulu's spot, but his new friend was gone. "Kulu?" he called. "Kulu, where are you?"

Silence.

Too much silence. Not even the cry of a bird or the lap of a wave broke it. Milo didn't dare breathe.

Then the ground rumbled.

Milo tried to catch his balance, but a wave from nowhere caught him behind the knees and dropped him on his bum.

He came up sputtering and rubbing his eyes. The sand shook beneath his homemade city. He watched in horror as a terrible monster burst from the ground…

And a thousand giant tentacles tore the sand city down.

Now Milo was upset. All that work, ruined!

Then he heard a sound like a dozen howling cats choking on sandpaper. He turned to find Kulu standing next to him. The monster was holding his belly and rocking back and forth – and the sounds were coming from *him*.

Kulu was *laughing*!

Milo didn't see what was so funny. "Kulu, did you do this?"

The creature nodded.

Milo started to say something, but he stopped before it came out. He watched Kulu giggling over his prank. How could he stay mad at that monstrous face?

He couldn't help it. He burst out laughing.

"That was so *cool*," Milo said, slapping Kulu's rock-hard shoulder. He was soon doubled over with mirth.

As his laughter subsided, Milo turned to the ruins of

their R'lyeh, and he sighed. "We'll have to rebuild it now."

Kulu shook like a dog, spraying sand from his tentacles. He looked at Milo's sad face, and back to their torn-down town.

Milo strode out of the water and knelt in the sand. He looked up at Kulu. "Will you help me?" Kulu shook his head. "Wha- why not?" Milo felt tears well up in his eyes. He angrily blinked them away. If Kulu didn't want to be his friend, then Milo didn't need him! He'd find another monster to play with.

Kulu's tentacle face writhed like it was forming words. "Nooooo…" the creature said.

"No what?"

"Noooo… neeeeetthhth."

Milo knocked the water out of his ears as Kulu repeated himself. "No… need?" Milo asked.

Kulu nodded.

"What do you mean?"

The octo-dragon raised a claw and pointed out to sea. "R'lyeh," he said.

Milo looked where Kulu pointed, then back at his

friend. "Riley?" he asked. "The city – the *real* city? It's out there?"

Kulu nodded again.

"*Wow…*" Milo's eyes grew wide. He sniffled and wiped his nose with the back of his hand; he'd already forgotten about his sadness. "Would you – could you – show it to me?"

The creature's tentacles formed a smile. "Yyyesssss…" he hissed.

Milo smiled back. "That is so *awesome.*"

Milo and Kulu walked up the beach to where Milo's parents had set up camp. Dad dozed beneath the umbrella. Mom sat in the other beach chair, wearing sunglasses and reading a romance novel on her smartphone.

"Mom," Milo said, "this is my new friend, Kulu."

Mom didn't look up. "That's nice, dear," she said. "Are you boys playing safe?"

"Oh yeah! We built a whole civilization in the sand. But then the Old Ones rose and destroyed it and devoured the souls of its people. So now we're gonna go to the city beneath the waves to wake the Shoggoth and the Deep Ones and prepare for the domination of this material plane."

Dad raised his head, looked at the boy, blinked at the squid-monster, stared out to sea for a moment, and went back to sleep.

"Okay," Mom said. "Have fun." She pursed her lips and eyed Milo over her phone. "But don't go too deep, now. And no throwing sand."

"No problem," Milo said.

"Good." Milo's Mom turned to Kulu. "Do your parents know where you are, young man?"

Kulu shrugged his massive shoulders and let his tentacles hang limp.

Mom frowned. "I'd rather your parents were informed you were having a play date," she said.

Milo huffed. He looked from his mother, to the sea monster's dejected face, and back again. "Mommm…" he whined.

"Milo, you know the rules," Mom replied. She turned to his new friend. "Now, as for you…"

Mom froze. She looked into Dread Cthulhu's black eyes and saw the horror of the Old Ones re-awakening, the powerlessness of human existence, the imminent end of space and time and the dawn of eternal insanity.

"Oh, alright," she said at last. Her expression

softened, and she smiled kindly. "Have fun, you two. And play safe!"

Milo grinned. "Thanks Mom!" he said. He turned and raced to the water, Kulu right on his heels.

They got to the edge of the beach, where the waves licked the sand and washed away the remains of their fallen castles. There they stopped.

Milo watched the sun touch the horizon, and he thought of R'lyeh. The sunken city of eternal night. Cyclopean masonry and sickening spheres and dimensions all wrong for this universe. He couldn't wait to see it. "Where dead Cthulhu waits dreaming," he whispered, though he didn't know why.

Kulu shook his head.

"Oh, right," Milo said with a giggle. "Not anymore!"

The octo-dragon smiled back. Then he raised his claws to the sky, spread his wings wide, and let his tentacles thrash in the breeze.

Milo saw the joy in his new friend's face, and it made him happy. "Are you ready?" he asked. He was almost bouncing himself.

With a gurgle of pleasure the monster marched into the sea. Milo laughed and ran splashing after him, waving his hands about and shouting for all the world to hear. Dread Cthulhu lifted the boy to his shoulders. Milo threw his arms up in triumph as the water rose.

They were soon lost to sight beneath the waves.

Hold onto your seats, brave reader!
Milo and Cthulhu return in:

CTHULHU 4 KIDS
BOOK II
RAISING R'LYEH

Available Now!

Here's a sneak preview to whet your appetite:

Milo and Kulu went beneath the waves.

They followed a clear path in the sand, going steadily deeper into the sea. Down and down they hiked, and down some more. It got darker the deeper they dove, but somehow Milo could still see. He could also still breathe, which seemed like a good thing.

Their road was surrounded by wonders.

They saw submarines and swordfish and sunken ships. They conversed with clams and crabs and corral sharks. They ate with alewives, danced with dragonfish, and sang with sea serpents.

The sights boggled Milo's brain. "Wow…" he said.

"Grrrlllppp…" Kulu agreed.

Milo made up a song on the spot, and soon he had the whole underwater world singing along with him:

Traveling down to meet the Shoggoth

Tra, la la, la laaaa

Waking the Old Ones from their sleep

Tra la la la, la laaa

Great darkness and the End of the World

Tra, la la, la laaaa

Down and down, we travel so deep

Tra la la la, la laaa

In the middle of the third verse, a Kraken grabbed Milo.

He yelped as the tentacle wrapped around his waist. It yanked him from the sandy sea bottom and pulled him toward an opening that must have been its mouth. "This is so *mean*!" Milo cried…

Will Milo escape???

Pick up *Cthulhu 4 Kids 2: Raising R'lyeh* (link below) **to find out what happens next!**

http://lukejmorris.com/book/cthulhu-4-kids-raising-rlyeh/

A Note to the Reader

Hi Reader!

We – Luke and Mo, that is – hope you really enjoyed this tale. If you did, would you (or your parents) kindly write it a review on the website where you purchased it? (If it was Amazon, go to this link: **http://amzn.to/1pDLWX5**)

Please do. We want to know what you think. If you tell us, we'll be your best friends forever.

And if you want some cool free stuff, join our mailing list at **lukejmorris.com/newsletter**. It's fun, we promise.

Are you looking forward to finding out what happens to Milo and Kulu on their visit to the sunken city of R'lyeh? Then pick up *Cthulhu 4 Kids II: Raising R'lyeh* at **lukejmorris.com/book/cthulhu-4-kids-raising-rlyeh/**! ☺

Thanks for reading!

About the Creators

Luke J. Morris is an author of adult fiction and non-fiction, as well as children's books like this one. When not writing, he teaches martial arts, hosts podcasts, sails sailboats, and improvises on stage. He's the proud father of 10-year-old Tyrion – a burgeoning author, artist, and H.P. Lovecraft fan in his own right. Visit Luke at:

www.lukejmorris.com

www.funwithfiction.com

Mo Simpson is an artist, actor, and podcast host. This is the second book he has illustrated with Luke (though the first that is appropriate for children). He is the proud papa of 1-year-old Miles, who will grow up with excellent taste in art and literature. See Mo at:

www.mozarknation.blogspot.com

www.eyeteeth.podbean.com

Made in the USA
San Bernardino, CA
17 April 2015